AF301844

Defoe
Abbott
Marx
Hardy
Melville
Montaigne
Machiavelli
Haggard
Chesterton
Cooper
Emerson
Joyce
Austen
Hugo
Eliot
Grimm
Stoker
Carroll
Christie
Molière
Wilde
Maupassant
Byron
Schiller
Garnett
Einstein
Fitzgerald
Engels
Goethe
Hawthorne
Smith
Kafka
Cotton
Dostoyevsky
Hall
Baum
Kipling
Doyle
Willis
Henry
Nietzsche
Leslie
Dumas
Flaubert
Turgenev
Balzac
Stockton
Vatsyayana
Crane
Burroughs
Verne
Curtis
Tocqueville
Gogol
Vinci
Homer
Widger
Tolstoy
Whitman
Busch
Darwin
Thoreau
Twain
Potter
Zola
Lawrence
Scott
Plato
Harte
Kant
Freud
Jowett
Stevenson
Dickens
London
Andersen
Descartes
Burton
Hesse
Poe
Aristotle
Wells
Cervantes
Voltaire
Hale
James
Hastings
Cooke
Bunner
Shakespeare
Irving
Richter
Chambers
Doré
Dante
Chekhov
Shaw
Wodehouse
Benedict
Alcott
Swift
Pushkin
Newton

The Banks of Wye

Robert Bloomfield

Imprint

This book is part of TREDITION CLASSICS

Author: Robert Bloomfield
Cover design: Buchgut, Berlin – Germany

Publisher: tredition GmbH, Hamburg - Germany
ISBN: 978-3-8424-6667-8

www.tredition.com
www.tredition.de

Copyright:
The content of this book is sourced from the public domain.

The intention of the TREDITION CLASSICS series is to make world literature in the public domain available in printed format. Literary enthusiasts and organizations, such as Project Gutenberg, worldwide have scanned and digitally edited the original texts. tredition has subsequently formatted and redesigned the content into a modern reading layout. Therefore, we cannot guarantee the exact reproduction of the original format of a particular historic edition. Please also note that no modifications have been made to the spelling, therefore it may differ from the orthography used today.

THE BANKS OF WYE;

A POEM.

In Four Books.

By ROBERT BLOOMFIELD,

Author of *The Farmer's Boy*.

London: Printed for the Author; Vernor, Hood, and Sharpe, Poultry; and Longman, Hurst, Rees, Orme, and Brown, Paternoster Row;

1811.

Printed by T. Hood and Co., St. John's Square, London.

To THOMAS LLOYD BAKER, ESQ.
Of Stout's Hill, Uley, And His Excellent Lady;
And
ROBERT BRANSBY COOPER, ESQ.
Of Ferwey Hill, Dursley, In The County Of Gloucester,
And All The Members Of His Family,
THIS JOURNAL IS DEDICATED,
With Sentiments Of High Esteem,
And A Lively Recollection Of Past Pleasures,
By Their Humble Servant,
THE AUTHOR.

PREFACE.

In the summer of 1807, a party of my good friends in Gloucestershire proposed to themselves a short excursion down the Wye, and through part of South Wales.

While this plan was in agitation, the lines which I had composed on "Shooter's Hill," during ill health, and inserted in my last volume, obtained their particular attention. A spirit of prediction, as well as sorrow, is there indulged; and it was now in the power of this happy party to falsify such predictions, and to render a pleasure to the writer of no common kind. An invitation to accompany them was the consequence; and the following Journal is the result of that invitation.

Should the reader, from being a resident, or frequent visitor, be well acquainted with the route, and able to discover inaccuracies in distances, succession of objects, or local particulars, he is requested to recollect, that the party was out but ten days; a period much too short for correct and laborious description, but quite sufficient for all the powers of poetry which I feel capable of exerting. The whole exhibits the language and feelings of a man who had never before seen a mountainous country; and of this it is highly necessary that the reader should be apprized.

A Swiss, or perhaps a Scottish Highlander, may smile at supposed or real exaggerations; but they will be excellent critics, when they call to mind that they themselves judge, in these cases, as I do, by comparison.

Perhaps it may be said, that because much of public approbation has fallen to my lot, it was unwise to venture again. I confess that the journey left such powerful, such unconquerable impressions on my mind, that embodying my thoughts in rhyme became a matter almost of necessity. To the parties concerned I know it will be an acceptable little volume: to whom, and to the public, it Is submitted with due respect.

ROBERT BLOOMFIELD.

City Road, London,

June 30,1811

THE BANKS OF WYE.

BOOK I.

CONTENTS OF BOOK I.

THE BANKS OF THE WYE.

BOOK I.

"Rouse from thy slumber, pleasure calls, arise,
Quit thy half-rural bower, awhile despise
The thraldom that consumes thee. We who dwell
Far from thy land of smoke, advise thee well.
Here Nature's bounteous hand around shall fling,
Scenes that thy Muse hath never dar'd to sing.
When sickness weigh'd thee down, and strength declin'd;
When dread eternity absorb'd thy mind,
Flow'd the predicting verse, by gloom o'erspread,
That 'Cambrian mountains' thou should'st never tread,
That 'time-worn cliff, and classic stream to see,'
Was wealth's prerogative, despair for thee.
Come to the proof; with us the breeze inhale,
Renounce despair, and come to Severn's vale;
And where the COTSWOLD HILLS are stretch'd along,
Seek our green dell, as yet unknown to song:
Start hence with us, and trace, with raptur'd eye,
The wild meanderings of the beauteous WYE;
Thy ten days leisure ten days joy shall prove,
And rock and stream breathe amity and love."

Such was the call; with instant ardour hail'd.
The syren Pleasure caroll'd and prevail'd;
Soon the deep dell appear'd, and the clear brow
Of ULEY BURY [A] smil'd o'er all below,
[Footnote A: Bury, or Burg, the Saxon name for a hill, particularly for
one wholly or partially formed by art.]
Mansion, and flock, and circling woods that hung
Round the sweet pastures where the sky-lark sung.

O for the fancy, vigorous and sublime,
Chaste as the theme, to triumph over time!
Bright as the rising day, and firm as truth,
To speak new transports to the lowland youth,
That bosoms still might throb, and still adore,
When his who strives to charm them beats no more!

One August morn, with spirits high,
Sound health, bright hopes, and cloudless sky,
A cheerful group their farewell bade
To DURSLEY tower, to ULEY'S shade;
And where bold STINCHCOMB'S greenwood side.
Heaves in the van of highland pride,
Scour'd the broad vale of Severn; there
The foes of verse shall never dare
Genius to scorn, or bound its power,
There blood-stain'd BERKLEY'S turrets low'r,
A name that cannot pass away,
Till time forgets "the Bard" of GRAY.

Quitting fair Glo'ster's northern road,
To gain the pass of FRAMELODE,
Before us DEAN'S black forest spread,
And MAY HILL, with his tufted head,
Beyond the ebbing tide appear'd;
And Cambria's distant mountains rear'd
Their dark blue summits far away;
And SEVERN, 'midst the burning day,
Curv'd his bright line, and bore along
The mingled *Avon*, pride of song.

The trembling steeds soon ferry'd o'er,
Neigh'd loud upon the forest shore;
Domains that once, at early morn,
Rang to the hunter's bugle horn,
When barons proud would bound away;
When even kings would hail the day,

And swell with pomp more glorious shows,
Than ant-hill population knows.
Here crested chiefs their bright-arm'd train
Of javelin'd horsemen rous'd amain,
And chasing wide the wolf or boar,
Bade the deep woodland vallies roar.

Harmless we past, and unassail'd,
Nor once at roads or tumpikes rail'd:
Through depths of shade oft sun-beams broke,
Midst noble FLAXLEY'S bowers of oak;
And many a cottage trim and gay,
Whisper'd delight through all the way;
On hills expos'd, in dells unseen,
To patriarchal MITCHEL DEAN.
Rose-cheek'd *Pomona* there was seen,
And *Ceres* edg'd her fields between,
And on each hill-top mounted high,
Her sickle wav'd in extasy;
Till Ross, thy charms all hearts confess'd,
Thy peaceful walks, thy hours of rest
And contemplation. Here the mind,
With all its luggage left behind,
Dame Affectation's leaden wares,
Spleen, envy, pride, life's thousand cares,
Feels all its dormant fires revive,
And sees "the *Man of Ross*" alive;
And hears the Twick'nham Bard again,
To KYRL'S high virtues lift his strain;
Whose own hand cloth'd this far-fam'd hill
With rev'rend elms, that shade us still;
Whose mem'ry shall survive the day,
When elms and empires feel decay.
KYRL die, by bard ennobled? Never;
"*The Man of Ross*" shall live for ever;
Ross, that exalts its spire on high,
Above the flow'ry-margin'd WYE,
Scene of the morrow's joy, that prest

Its unseen beauties on our rest
In dreams; but who of dreams would tell,
Where truth sustains the song so well?

The morrow came, and Beauty's eye
Ne'er beam'd upon a lovelier sky;
Imagination instant brought,
And dash'd amidst the train of thought,
Tints of the bow. The boatman stript;
Glee at the helm exulting tript,
And way'd her flower-encircled wand,
"Away, away, to Fairy Land."
Light dipt the oars; but who can name
The various objects dear to fame,
That changing, doubting, wild, and strong,
Demand the noblest powers of song?
Then, O forgive the vagrant Muse,
Ye who the sweets of Nature choose;
And thou whom destiny hast tied
To this romantic river's side,
Down gazing from each close retreat,
On boats that glide beneath thy feet,
Forgive the stranger's meagre line,
That seems to slight that spot of thine;
For he, alas! could only glean
The changeful outlines of the scene;
A momentary bliss; and here
Links memory's power with rapture's tear.

Who curb'd the barons' kingly power[A]? [Footnote A: Henry the
Seventh gave an irrevocable blow to the dangerous privileges as-
sumed by the barons, in abolishing liveries and retainers, by which
every malefactor could shelter himself from the law, on assuming a
nobleman's livery, and attending his person. And as a finishing
stroke to the feudal tenures, an act was passed, by which the barons
and gentlemen of landed interest were at liberty to sell and mort-
gage their lands, without fines or licences for the alienation.] Let
hist'ry tell that fateful hour At home, when surly winds shall roar,

And prudence shut the study door. DE WILTON'S here of mighty
name, The whelming flood, the summer stream, Mark'd from their
towers. — The fabric falls, The rubbish of their splendid halls, Time
in his march hath scatter'd wide, And blank oblivion strives to hide.

Awhile the grazing herd was seen,
And trembling willow's silver green,
Till the fantastic current stood,
In line direct for PENCRAIG WOOD;
Whose bold green summit welcome bade,
Then rear'd behind his nodding shade.
Here, as the light boat skimm'd along,
The clarionet, and chosen song,
That mellow, wild, Eolian lay,
"Sweet in the Woodlands," roll'd away,
In echoes down the stream, that bore
Each dying close to every shore,
And forward Cape, and woody range,
That form the never-ceasing change,
To him who floating, void of care,
Twirls with the stream, he knows not where;
Till bold, impressive, and sublime,
Gleam'd all that's left by storms and time
Of GOODRICH TOWERS. The mould'ring pile
Tells noble truths, — but dies the while;
O'er the steep path, through brake and briar,
His batter'd turrets still aspire,
In rude magnificence. 'Twas here
LANCASTRIAN HENRY spread his cheer,
When came the news that HAL was born,
And MONMOUTH hail'd th' auspicious morn;
A boy in sports, a prince in war,
Wisdom and valour crown'd his car;
Of France the terror, England's glory,
As Stratford's bard has told the story.

No butler's proxies snore supine,
Where the old monarch kept his wine;
No Welch ox roasting, horns and all,

Adorns his throng'd and laughing hall;
But where he pray'd, and told his beads,
A thriving ash luxuriant spreads.

No wheels by piecemeal brought the pile;
No barks embowel'd Portland Isle;
Dig, cried experience, dig away,
Bring the firm quarry into day,
The excavation still shall save
Those ramparts which its entrails gave.
"Here kings shall dwell," the builders cried;
"Here England's foes shall low'r their pride;
Hither shall suppliant nobles come,
And this be England's royal home."
Vain hope! for on the Gwentian shore,
The regal banner streams no more!
Nettles, and vilest weeds that grow,
To mock poor grandeur's head laid low,
Creep round the turrets valour rais'd,
And flaunt where youth and beauty gaz'd.

Here fain would strangers loiter long,
And muse as Fancy's woof grows strong;
Yet cold the heart that could complain,
Where POLLETT [Footnote: The boatman.] struck his oars again;
For lovely as the sleeping child,
The stream glides on sublimely wild,
In perfect beauty, perfect ease;
The awning trembled in the breeze,
And scarcely trembled, as we stood
For RUERDEAN Spire, and BISHOP'S WOOD.
The fair domains of COURTFIELD [A] made
A paradise of mingled shade
[Footnote A: A seat belonging to the family of Vaughan, which is
not
unnoticed in the pages of history. According to tradition, it is the
place
where Henry the Fifth was nursed, under the care of the Countess

of
Salisbury, from which circumstance the original name of Grayfield
is said
to have been changed to Courtfield. (This is probably an erroneous
tradition; for Court was a common name for a manor-house, where
the lord
of the manor held his court. —*Core's Monmouth*.)]
Round BICKNOR'S tiny church, that cowers
Beneath his host of woodland bowers.

But who the charm of words shall fling,
O'er RAVEN CLIFF and COLDWELL Spring,
To brighten the unconscious eye,
And wake the soul to extasy?

Noon scorch'd the fields; the boat lay to;
The dripping oars had nought to do,
Where round us rose a scene that might
Enchant an ideot — glorious sight!
Here, in one gay according mind,
Upon the sparkling stream we din'd;
As shepherds free on mountain heath,
Free as the fish that watch'd beneath
For falling crumbs, where cooling lay
The wine that cheer'd us on our way.
Th' unruffled bosom of the stream,
Gave every tint and every gleam;
Gave shadowy rocks, and clear blue sky,
And double clouds of various dye;
Gave dark green woods, or russet brown,
And pendant corn-fields, upside down.

A troop of gleaners chang'd their shade,
And 'twas a change by music made;
For slowly to the brink they drew,
To mark our joy, and share it too.
How oft, in childhood's flow'ry days,

I've heard the wild impassion'd lays
Of such a group, lays strange and new,
And thought, was ever song so true?
When from the hazel's cool retreat,
They watch'd the summer's trembling heat;
And through the boughs rude urchins play'd,
Where matrons, round the laughing maid,
Prest the long grass beneath! And here
They doubtless shar'd an equal cheer;
Enjoy'd the feast with equal glee,
And rais'd the song of revelry:
Yet half abash'd reserv'd, and shy,
Watch'd till the strangers glided by.

GLEANER'S SONG

Dear Ellen, your tales are all plenteously stor'd,
With the joys of some bride, and the wealth of her lord.
   Of her chariots and dresses,
   And worldly caresses,
And servants that fly when she's waited upon:
But what can she boast if she weds unbelov'd?
Can she e'er feel the joy that one morning I prov'd,
When I put on my new gown and waited for John?

These fields, my dear Ellen, I knew them of yore,
Yet to me they ne'er look'd so enchanting before;
   The distant bells ringing,
   The birds round us singing,
For pleasure is pure when affection is won;
They told me the troubles and cares of a wife;
But I lov'd him; and that was the pride of my life,
When I put on my new gown and waited for John.

He shouted and ran, as he leapt from the stile;
And what in my bosom was passing the while?
   For love knows the blessing
   Of ardent caressing,
When virtue inspires us, and doubts are all gone.
The sunshine of Fortune you say is divine;
True love and the sunshine of Nature were mine,
When I put on my new gown and waited for John.

Never could spot be suited less
To bear memorials of distress;
None, cries the sage, more fit is found,
They strike at once a double wound;
Humiliation bids you sigh,

And think of immortality.

Close on the bank, and half o'ergrown,
Beneath a dark wood's soinbrous frown,
A monumental stone appears,
Of one who in his blooming years,
While bathing spurn'd the grassy shore,
And sunk, midst friends, to rise no more;
By parents witness'd — Hark! their shrieks!
The dreadful language horror speaks!
But why in verse attempt to tell
That tale the stone records so well[A]?

[Footnote A: *Inscription on the side towards the water*. "Sacred to the memory of JOHN WHITEHEAD WARRE, who perished near this spot, whilst bathing in the river Wye, in sight of his afflicted parents, brother, and sister, on the 11th of September, 1804, in the sixteenth year of his age.

GOD'S WILL BE DONE,

"Who, in his mercy, hath granted consolation to the parents of the dear departed, in the reflection, that he possessed truth, innocence, filial piety, and fraternal affection, in the highest degree. That, but a few moments before he was called to a better life, he had (with a never to be forgotten piety) joined his family in joyful thanks to his Maker, for the restoration of his mother's health. His parents, in justice to his amiable virtue, and excellent disposition, declare, that he was void of offence towards them. With humbled hearts they bow to the Almighty's dispensation; trusting, through the mediation of his blessed Son, he will mercifully receive their child he so suddenly took to himself.

"This monument is here erected to warn parents and others how they trust the deceitful stream; and particularly to exhort them to learn and observe the directions of the Humane Society, for the recovery of persons apparently drowned. Alas! it is with the extremest sorrow here commemorated, what anguish is felt from a want of this knowledge. The lamented swam very well; was endowed with great bodily strength and activity; and possibly, had proper application been used, might have been saved from his untimely fate. He was born at Oporto, in the kingdom of Portugal, on the 14th of February, 1789; third son of James Warre, of London, and of the county of Somerset, merchant, and Elinor, daughter of Thomas Gregg, of Belfast, Esq.

"Passenger, whoever thou art, spare this tomb! It is erected for the benefit of the surviving, being but a poor record of the grief of those who witnessed the sad occasion of it. God preserve you and yours from such calamity! May you not require their assistance; but if you should, the apparatus, with directions for the application by the Humane Society, for the saving of persons apparently drowned, are lodged at the church of Coldwell."

On the opposite side is inscribed "It is with gratitude acknowledged by the parents of the deceased, that permission was gratuitously, and most obligingly, granted for the erection of this monument, by William Vaughan, Esq. of Courtfield."]

Nothing could damp th'awaken'd joy,
Not e'en thy fate, ingenuous boy;
The great, the grand of Nature strove,
To lift our hearts to life and love.
HAIL! COLDWELL ROCKS; frown, frown away;
Thrust from your woods your shafts of gray:
Fall not, to crush our mortal pride,
Or stop the stream on which we glide.
Our lives are short, our joys are few;
But, giants, what is time to you?
Ye who erect, in many a mass,
Rise from the scarcely dimpled glass,
That with distinct and mellow glow,
Reflect your monstrous forms below;
Or in clear shoals, in breeze or sun,
Shake all your shadows into one;
Boast ye o'er man in proud disdain,
An everlasting silent reign?
Bear ye your heads so high in scorn
Of names that puny man hath borne?

Would that the Cambrian bards had here
Their names carv'd deep, so deep, so clear,
That such as gaily wind along,
Might shout and cheer them with a song;
Might rush on wings of bliss away,
Through Fancy's boundless blaze of day!

Not nameless quite ye lift your brows,
For each the navigator knows;
Not by King Arthur, or his knights,
Bard faim'd in lays, or chief in fights:
But former tourists, just us free,
(Tho' surely not so blest as we,)
Mark'd towering BEARCROFT'S ivy crown,
And grey VANSITTART'S waving gown:
And who's that giant by his side?
"SERGEANT ADAIR," the boatman cried.
Strange may it seem, however true,
That here, where law has nought to do,
Where rules and bonds are set aside,
By wood, by rock, by stream defy'd;
That here, where nature seems at strife
With all that tells of busy life,
Man should by *names* be carried still,
To Babylon against his will.

But how shall memory rehearse,
Or dictate the untoward verse
That truth demands? Could he refuse
Thy unsought honours, darling Muse,
He who in idle, happy trim,
Rode just where friends would carry him?
Truth, I obey.—The generous band,
That spread his board and grasp'd his hand,
In native mirth, as here they came,
Gave a bluff rock *his* humble name:
A yew-tree clasps its rugged base;
The boatman knows its reverend face;

And with his *memory* and his *fee*,
Rests the result that time shall see.
Yet e'en if time shall sweep away
The fragile whimsies of a day;
Or travellers rest the dashing oar,
To hear the mingled echoes roar;
A stranger's triumph — he will feel
A joy that death alone can steal.
And should he cold indifference feign,
And treat such honours with disdain,
Pretending pride shall not deceive him,
Good people all, pray don't believe him;
In such a spot to leave a name,
At least is no opprobrious fame;
This rock perhaps uprear'd his brow,
Ere human blood began to flow.

And let not wandering strangers fear
That WYE is ended there or here;
Though foliage close, though hills may seem
To bar all access to a stream,
Some airy height he climbs amain,
And finds the silver eel again.
  No fears we form'd, no labours counted,
Yet SYMMON'S YAT must be surmounted;
A tower of rock that seems to cry,
'Go round about me, neighbour WYE[A].'
[Footnote A: This rocky isthmus, perforated at the base, would measure not
more than six hundred yards, and its highest point is two thousand feet
above the water. If this statement, taken from Coxe's History of
Monmouthshire, and an Excursion down the Wye, by C. Heath, of Monmouth, is
correct, its elevation is greater than that of the "Pen-y-Vale," or the
"Sugar-Loaf Hill," near Abergavenny. Yet it has less the appearance of a
mountain, than the river has that of an excavation.]

On went the boat, and up the steep
Her straggling crew began to creep,
To gain the ridge, enjoy the view,
Where the the pure gales of summer blew.
The gleaming WYE, that circles round
Her four-mile course, again is found;
And crouching to the conqueror's pride,
Bathes his huge cliffs on either side;
Seen at one glance, when from his brow,
The eye surveys twin gulphs below.

Whence comes thy name? What *Symon* he,
Who gain'd a monument in thee?
Perhaps a rude woodhunter, born
Peril, and toil, and death, to scorn;
Or warrior, with his powerful lance,
Who scal'd the cliff to gain a glance;
Or shepherd lad, or humble swain,
Who sought for pasture here in vain;
Or venerable bard, who strove
To tune his harp to themes of love;
Or with a poet's ardent flame,
Sung to the winds his country's fame?

Westward GREAT DOWARD, stretching wide,
Upheaves his iron-bowel'd side;
And by his everlasting mound,
Prescribes th' imprison'd river's bound,
And strikes the eye with mountain force:
But stranger mark thy rugged course
From crag to crag, unwilling, slow,
To NEW WIER forge that smokes below.
Here rush'd the keel like lightning by;
The helmsman watch'd with anxious eye;
And oars alternate touch'd the brim,
To keep the flying boat in trim.

[Illustration: NEW WEAR on the WYE]

Hush! not a whisper! Oars, be still!
Comes that soft sound from yonder hill?
Or is it close at hand, so near
It scarcely strikes the list'ning ear?
E'en so; for down the green bank fell,
An ice-cold stream from Martin's Well,
Bright as young beauty's azure eye,
And pure as infant chastity,
Each limpid draught, suffus'd with dew,
The dipping glass's crystal hue;
And as it trembling reach'd the lip,
Delight sprung up at every sip.

Pure, temperate joys, and calm, were these;
We tost upon no Indian seas;
No savage chiefs, of various hue,
Came jabbering in the bark canoe
Our strength to dare, our course to turn;
Yet boats a South Sea chief would burn[A],
[Footnote A: In Caesar's Commentaries, mention is made of boats of
this
description, formed of a raw hide, (from whence, perhaps, their
name
Coricle,) which were in use among the natives. How little they
dreamed of
the vastnss of modern perfection, and of the naval conflicts of latter
days!]
Sculk'd in the alder shade. Each bore,
Devoid of keel, or sail, or oar,
An upright fisherman, whose eye,
With Bramin-like solemnity,
Survey'd the surface either way,
And cleav'd it like a fly at play;
And crossways bore a balanc'd pole,
To drive the salmon from his hole;
Then heedful leapt, without parade,
On shore, as luck or fancy bade;

And o'er his back, in gallant trim,
Swung the light shell that carried him;
Then down again his burden threw,
And launch'd his whirling bowl anew;
Displaying, in his bow'ry station,
The infancy of navigation.

Soon round us spread the hills and dales,
Where GEOFFREY spun his magic tales,
And call'd them history. The land
Whence ARTHUR sprung, and all his band
Of gallant knights. Sire of romance,
Who led the fancy's mazy dance,
Thy tales shall please, thy name still be,
When Time forgets my verse and me.

Low sunk the sun, his ev'ning beam
Scarce reach'd us on the tranquil stream;
Shut from the world, and all its din,
Nature's own bonds had clos'd us in;
Wood, and deep dell, and rock, and ridge,
From smiling Ross to Monmouth Bridge;
From morn, till twilight stole away,
A long, unclouded, glorious day.

END OF THE FIRST BOOK.

THE BANKS OF WYE

BOOK II

CONTENTS OF BOOK II.

BOOK II.

HARRY of MONMOUTH, o'er thy page,
Great chieftain of a daring age,
The stripling soldier burns to see
The spot of thy nativity;
His ardent fancy can restore
Thy castle's turrets, now no more;
See the tall plumes of victory wave,
And call old valour from the grave;
Twang the strong bow, and point the lance,
That pierc'd the shatter'd hosts of France,
When Europe, in the days of yore,
Shook at the rampant lion's roar.

Ten hours were all we could command;
The Boat was moor'd upon the strand,
The midnight current, by her side,
Was stealing down to meet the tide;
The wakeful steersman ready lay,
To rouse us at the break of day;
It came — how soon! and what a sky,

To cheer the bounding traveller's eye!
To make him spurn his couch of rest,
To shout upon the river's breast;
Watching by turns the rosy hue
Of early cloud, or sparkling dew;
These living joys the verse shall tell,
Harry, and Monmouth, fare-ye-well.

On upland farm, and airy height,
Swept by the breeze, and cloth'd in light,
The reapers, early from their beds,
Perhaps were singing o'er our heads.
For, stranger, deem not that the eye
Could hence survey the eastern sky;
Or mark the streak'd horizon's bound,
Where first the rosy sun wheels round;
Deep in the gulf beneath were we,
Whence climb'd blue mists o'er rock and tree;
A mingling, undulating crowd,
That form'd the dense or fleecy cloud;
Slow from the darken'd stream upborne,
They caught the quick'ning gales of morn;
There bade their parent WYE good day,
And ting'd with purple sail'd away.

The MUNNO join'd us all unseen,
TROY HOUSE, and BEAUFORT'S bowers of green,
And nameless prospects, half defin'd,
Involv'd in mist, were left behind.
Yet as the boat still onward bore,
These ramparts of the eastern shore
Cower'd the high crest to many a sweep,
And bade us o'er each minor steep
Mark the bold KYMIN'S sunny brow,
That, gleaming o'er our fogs below,
Lifted amain with giant power,
E'en to the clouds his NAVAL TOWER[1];
[Footnote 1: The Kymin Pavilion, erected in honour of the British

Admirals, and their unparalleled victories.]
Proclaiming to the morning sky,
Valour, and fame, and victory.

The air resign'd its hazy blue,
Just as LANDOGA came in view;
Delightful village! one by one,
Its climbing dwellings caught the sun.
So bright the scene, the air so clear,
Young Love and Joy seem'd station'd here;
And each with floating banners cried,
"Stop friends, you'll meet the slimy tide."

Rude fragments, torn, disjointed, wild,
High on the Glo'ster shore are pil'd;
No ruin'd fane, the boast of years,
Unstain'd by time the group appears;
With foaming wrath, and hideous swell,
Brought headlong down a woodland dell,
When a dark thunder-storm had spread
Its terrors round the guilty head;
When rocks, earth-bound, themselves gave way,
When crash'd the prostrate timbers lay.
O, it had been a noble sight,
Crouching beyond the torrent's might,
To mark th' uprooted victims bow,
The grinding masses dash below,
And hear the long deep peal the while
Burst over TINTERN'S roofless pile!
Then, as the sun regain'd his power,
When the last breeze from hawthorn bower,
Or Druid oak, had shook away
The rain-drops 'midst the gleaming day,
Perhaps the sigh of hope return'd
And love in some chaste bosom burn'd,
And softly trill'd the stream along,
Some rustic maiden's village song.

The Maid of Landoga.

Return, my Llewellyn, the glory
That heroes may gain o'er the sea,
  Though nations may feel
  Their invincible steel,
By falsehood is tarnish'd in story;
Why tarry, Llewellyn, from me?

Thy sails, on the fathomless ocean,
Are swell'd by the boisterous gale;
  How rests thy tir'd head
  On the rude rocking bed?
While here not a leaf is in motion,
And melody reigns in the dale.

The mountains of Monmouth invite thee;
The WYE, O how beautiful here!
  This woodbine, thine own,
  Hath the cottage o'ergrown,
O what foreign shore can delight thee,
And where is the current so clear?

Can lands where false pleasure assails thee,
And beauty invites thee to roam;
  Can the deep orange grove
  Charm with shadows of love?
Thy love at LANDOGA bewails thee;
Remember her truth and thy home.

Adieu, LANDOGA, scene most dear,
Farewell we bade to ETHEL'S WIER;
Round many a point then bore away,
Till morn was chang'd to beauteous day:
And forward on the lowland shore,
Silent majestic ruins wore
The stamp of holiness; this strand

The steersman hail'd, and touch'd the land.

SUDDEN the change; at once to tread
The grass-grown mansions of the dead!
Awful to feeling, where, immense,
Rose ruin'd, gray magnificence;
The fair-wrought shaft all ivy-bound,
The tow'ring arch with foliage crown'd,
That trembles on its brow sublime,
Triumphant o'er the spoils of time.
Here, grasping all the eye beheld,
Thought into mingling anguish swell'd.
And check'd the wild excursive wing,
O'er dust or bones of priest or king;
Or rais'd some STRONGBOW[A] warrior's ghost
To shout before his banner'd host.
[Footnote A: They shew here a mutilated figure, which they call the famous
Earl Strongbow; but it appears from Coxe that he was buried at Gloucester.]
But all was still. — The chequer'd floor
Shall echo to the step no more;
Nor airy roof the strain prolong,
Of vesper chant or choral song.

TINTERN, thy name shall hence sustain
A thousand raptures in my brain;
Joys, full of soul, all strength, all eye,
That cannot fade, that cannot die.

No loitering here, lone walks to steal,
Welcome the early hunter's meal;
For time and tide, stern couple, ran
Their endless race, and laugh'd at man;
Deaf, had we shouted, "turn about?"
Or, "wait a while, till we come out;"
To humour them we check'd our pride,

And ten cheer'd hearts stow'd side by side;
Push'd from the shore with current strong,
And, "Hey for Chepstow," steer'd along.

Amidst the bright expanding day,
Solemnly deep, dark shadows lay,
Of that rich foliage, tow'ring o'er
Where princely abbots dwelt of yore.
The mind, with instantaneous glance,
Beholds his barge of state advance,
Borne proudly down the ebbing tide,
She turns the waving boughs aside;
She winds with flowing pendants drest,
And as the current turns south-west,
She strikes her oars, where full in view,
Stupendous WIND-CLIFF greets his crew.
But, Fancy, let thy day-dreams cease,
With fallen greatness be at peace;
Enough; for WIND-CLIFF still was found
To hail us as we doubled round.

Bold in primeval strength he stood;
His rocky brow, all shagg'd with wood,
O'er-look'd his base, where, doubling strong,
The inward torrent pours along;
Then ebbing turns, and turns again,
To meet the Severn and the Main,
Beneath the dark shade sweeping round,
Of beetling PERSFIELD'S fairy ground,
By buttresses of rock upborne,
The rude APOSTLES all unshorn.

Long be the slaught'ring axe defy'd;
Long may they bear their waving pride;
Tree over tree, bower over bower,
In uncurb'd nature's wildest power;
Till WYE forgets to wind below,

And genial spring to bid them grow.

And shall we e'er forget the day, When our last chorus died away? When first we hail'd, then moor'd beside Rock-founded CHEPSTOW'S mouldering pride? Where that strange bridge[1], light, trembling, high, Strides like a spider o'er the WYE; [Footnote 1: "On my arrival at Chepstow," says Mr. Coxe, "I walked to the bridge; it was low water, and I looked down on the river ebbing between forty and fifty feet beneath; six hours after it rose near forty feet, almost reached the floor of the bridge, and flowed upward with great rapidity. The channel in this place being narrow in proportion to the Severn, and confined between perpendicular cliffs, the great rise and fall of the river are peculiarly manifest."] When, for the joys the morn had giv'n, Our thankful hearts were rais'd to heav'n? Never; — that moment shall be dear, While hills can charm, or sun-beams cheer.

Pollett, farewell! Thy dashing oar
Shall lull us into peace no more;
But where Kyrl trimm'd his infant green,
Long mayst thou with thy bark be seen;
And happy be the hearts that glide
Through such a scene, with such a guide.

The verse of gravel walks that tells,
With pebble rocks and mole-hill swells,
May strain description's bursting cheeks,
And far out-run the goal it seeks.
Not so when ev'ning's purpling hours,
Hied us away to Persfield bowers:
Here no such danger waits the lay,
Sing on, and truth shall lead the way;
Here sight may range, and hearts may glow,
Yet shrink from the abyss below;
Here echoing precipices roar,
As youthful ardour shouts before;
Here a sweet paradise shall rise
At once to greet poetic eyes.

Then why does he dispel, unkind,
The sweet illusion from the mind,
That giant, with the goggling eye,
Who strides in mock sublimity?
Giants, identified, may frown,
Nature and taste would knock them down:
Blocks that usurp some noble station,
As if to curb imagination,
That, smiling at the chissel's pow'r,
Makes better monsters erery hour.

Beneath impenetrable green,
Down 'midst the hazel stems was seen
The turbid stream, with all that past;
The lime-white deck, the gliding mast;
Or skiff with gazers darting by,
Who rais'd their hands in extasy.
Impending cliffs hung overhead;
The rock-path sounded to the tread,
Where twisted roots, in many a fold,
Through moss, disputed room for hold.

The stranger thus who steals one hour
To trace thy walks from bower to bower,
Thy noble cliffs, thy wildwood joys,
Nature's own work that never cloys,
Who, while reflection bids him roam,
Exclaims not, "PERSFIELD is my *home*"
Can ne'er, with dull unconscious eye,
Leave them behind without a sigh.
Thy tale of truth then, Sorrow, tell,
Of one who bade *this home* farewell;
MORRIS of PERSFIELD. — Hark, the strains!
Hark! 'tis some Monmouth bard complains!
The deeds, the worth, he knew so well,
The force of nature bids him tell.

MORRIS OF PERSFIELD

Who was lord of yon beautiful seat;
  Yon woods which are tow'ring so high?
Who spread the rich board for the great,
  Yet listen'd to pity's soft sigh?

Who gave alms with a spirit so free?
  Who succour'd distress at his door?
Our Morris of Persfield was he,
  Who dwelt in the hearts of the poor.

But who e'en of wealth shall make sure,
  Since wealth to misfortune has bow'd?
Long cherish'd untainted and pure,
  The stream of his charity flow'd.
But all his resources gave way,
  O what could his feelings controul?
What shall curb, in the prosperous day,
  Th' excess of a generous soul?

He bade an adieu to the town,
  O, can I forget the sad day?
When I saw the poor widows kneel down,
  To bless him, to weep, and to pray.

Though sorrow was mark'd in his eye,
  This trial he manfully bore;
Then pass'd o'er the bridge of the WYE,
  To return to his PERSFIELD no more.

Yet surely another may feel,
  And poverty still may be fed;
I was one who rung out the dumb peal,

For to us noble MORRIS was dead.
He had not lost sight of his home,
  Yon domain that so lovely appears,
When he heard it, and sunk overcome;
  He could feel, and he burst into tears.

The lessons of prudence have charms,
  And slighted, may lead to distress;
But the man whom benevolence warms,
  Is an angel who lives but to bless.

    If ever man merited fame, If ever man's failings went free, Forgot at the sound of his name, Our Morris of Persfield was he[1]. [Footnote 1: The author is equally indebted to Mr. Coxe's County History for this anecdote, as for the greater part of the notes subjoined throughout the Journal.]

CLEFT from the summit, who shall say
When WIND-CLIFF'S other half gave way?
Or when the sea-waves roaring strong,
First drove the rock-bound tide along?
To studious leisure be resign'd,
The task that leads the wilder'd mind
From time's first birth throughout the range
Of Nature's everlasting change.
Soon from his all-commanding brow,
Lay PERSFIELD'S rocks and woods below.

Back over MONMOUTH who could trace
The WYE'S fantastic mountain race?
Before us, sweeping far and wide.
Lay out-stretch'd SEVERN'S ocean tide,
Through whose blue mists, all upward blown,
Broke the faint lines of heights unknown;
And still, though clouds would interpose,
The COTSWOLD promontories rose
In dark succession: STINCHCOMB'S brow,
With BERKLEY CASTLE crouch'd below;

And stranger spires on either hand,
From THORNBURY, on the Glo'ster strand;
With black-brow'd woods, and yellow fields,
The boundless wealth that summer yields,
Detain'd the eye, that glanc'd again
O'er KINGROAD anchorage to the main.

Or was the bounded view preferr'd,
Far, far beneath the spreading herd
Low'd as the cow-boy stroll'd along,
And cheerly sung his last new song.
But cow-boy, herd, and tide, and spire,
Sunk Into gloom, the tinge of fire,
As westward roll'd the setting day,
Fled like a golden dream away.
Then CHEPSTOW'S ruin'd fortress caught
The mind's collected store of thought,
And seem'd, with mild but jealous frown,
To promise peace, and warn us down.
Twas well; for he has much to boast,
Much still that tells of glories lost,
Though rolling years have form'd the sod,
Where once the bright-helm'd warrior trod
From tower to tower, and gaz'd around,
While all beneath him slept profound.
E'en on the walls where pac'd the brave,
High o'er his crumbling turrets wave
The rampant seedlings—Not a breath
Past through their leaves; when, still as death,
We stopp'd to watch the clouds—for night
Grew splendid with encreasing light,
Till, as time loudly told the hour,
Gleam'd the broad front of MARTEN'S TOWER[1],
[Footnote 1: Henry Marten, whose signature appears upon the
death-warrant
of Charles the First, finished his days here in prison. Marten lived to
the advanced age of seventy-eight, and died by a stroke of apo-
plexy, which

seized him while he was at dinner, in the twentieth year of his
confinement. He was buried in the chancel of the parish church at
Chepstow. Over his ashes was placed a stone with an inscription,
which
remained there until one of the succeeding vicars declaring his ab-
horrence
that the monument of a rebel should stand so near the altar, re-
moved the
stone into the body of the church!]

[Illustration: Marten's Tower, Chepstow Castle.]

Bright silver'd by the moon. — Then rose
The wild notes sacred to repose;
Then the lone owl awoke from rest,
Stretch'd his keen talons, plum'd his crest,
And from his high embattl'd station,
Hooted a trembling salutation.
Rocks caught the "halloo" from his tongue,
And PERSFIELD back the echoes flung
Triumphant o'er th' illustrious dead,
Their history lost, their glories fled.

END OF THE SECOND BOOK.

BOOK III.

CONTENTS OF BOOK III.

Departure for Ragland. — Ragland Castle. — Abergavenny. —
Expedition up the
"Pen-y-Vale," or Sugar-Loaf Hill. — Invocation to the Spirit of
Burns. —

View from the Mountain. — Castle of Abergaveuny. — Departure for Brecon. —
Pembrokes of Crickbowel — Tre-Tower Castle. — Jane Edwards.

THE BANKS OF WYE.

BOOK III.

PEACE to your white-wall'd cots, ye vales,
Untainted fly your summer gales;
Health, thou from cities lov'st to roam,
O make the Monmouth hills your home!
Great spirits of her bards of yore,
While harvests triumph, torrents roar,
Train her young shepherds, train them high
To sing of mountain liberty:
Give them the harp and modest maid;
Give them the sacred village shade.
Long be Llandenny, and Llansoy,
Names that import a rural joy;
Known to our fathers, when May-day
Brush'd a whole twelvemonth's cares away.

Oft on the lisping infant's tongue
Reluctant information hung,
Till, from a belt of woods full grown,
Arose immense thy turrets brown,
Majestic RAGLAND! Harvests wave
Where thund'ring hosts their watch-word gave,
When cavaliers, with downcast eye,
Struck the last flag of loyalty[1]:
[Footnote 1: This castle, with a garrison commanded by the Marquis of
Worcester, was the last place of strength which held out for the
unfortunate Charles the First.]
Then, left by gallant WORC'STER'S band,
To devastation's cruel hand
The beauteous fabric bow'd, fled all
The splendid hours of festival.
No smoke ascends; the busy hum

Is heard no more; no rolling drum,
No high-ton'd clarion sounds alarms,
No banner wakes the pride of arms[A];
[Footnote A: "These magnificent ruins, including the citadel, occupy
a tract of ground not less than one-third of a mile in circumference."
"In addition to the injury the castle sustained from the parliamen-
tary
army, considerable dilapidations have been occasioned by the nu-
merous
tenants in the vicinity, who conveyed away the stone and other
materials
for the construction of farm-houses, barns, and other buildings. No
less
than twenty-three staircases were taken down by these devastators;
but the
present Duke of Beanfort no sooner succeeded to his estate, than he
instantly gave orders that not a stone should be moved from its
situation,
and thus preserved these noble ruins from destruction."
History of Monmouthshire, page 148.]
But ivy, creeping year by year,
Of growth enormous, triumphs here.
Each dark festoon with pride upheaves
Its glossy wilderness of leaves
On sturdy limbs, that, clasping, bow
Broad o'er the turrets utmost brow,
Encompassing, by strength alone,
In tret-work bars, the sliding stone,
That tells how years and storms prevail,
And spreads its dust upon the gale.

The man who could unmov'd survey
What ruin, piecemeal, sweeps away;
Works of the pow'rful and the brave,
All sleeping in the silent grave;
Unmov'd reflect that here were sung
Carols of joy, by beauty's tongue,
Is fit, where'er he deigns to roam,

And hardly fit—to stay at home.
Spent here in peace one solemn hour,
'Midst legends of the YELLOW TOWER,
Truth and tradition's mingled stream,
Fear's start, and superstition's dream[1]
[Footnote 1: A village woman, who very officiously pointed out all that
she knew respecting the former state of the castle, desired us to remark
the descent to a vault, apparently of large dimensions, in which she had
heard that no candle would continue burning; "and," added she, "they say
it is because of the damps; but for my part, I think the devil is there."]
Is pregnant with a thousand joys,
That distance, place, nor time destroys;
That with exhaustless stores supply
Food for reflection till we die.

ONWARD the rested steeds pursu'd
The cheerful route, with strength renew'd,
For onward lay the gallant town,
Whose name old custom hath clipp'd down,
With more of music left than many,
So handily to ABERGANY.
And as the sidelong, sober light
Left valleys darken'd, hills less bright,
Great BLORENGE rose to tell his tale;
And the dun peak of PEN-Y-VALE
Stood like a centinel, whose brow
Scowl'd on the sleeping world below;
Yet even sleep itself outspread
The mountain paths we meant to tread,
'Midst fresh'ning gales all unconfin'd,
Where USK'S broad valley shrinks behind.

Joyous the crimson morning rose,
As joyous from the night's repose
Sprung the light heart, the glancing eye
Beheld, amidst the dappl'd sky,
Exulting PEN-Y-VALE. But how
Could females climb his gleaming brow,
Rude toil encount'ring? how defy
The wintry torrent's course, when dry,
A rough-scoop'd bed of stones? or meet
The powerful force of August heat?
Wheels might assist, could wheels be found
Adapted to the rugged ground:
'Twas done; for prudence bade us start
With three Welch ponies, and a cart;
A red-cheek'd mountaineer[A], a wit,
Full of rough shafts, that sometimes hit,
[Footnote A: The driver, Powell, I believe, occupied a cottage, or small
farm, which we past during the ascent, and where goats milk was offered
for refreshment.]
Trudg'd by their side, and twirl'd his thong,
And cheer'd his scrambling team along.

At ease to mark a scene so fair,
And treat their steeds with mountain air,
Some rode apart, or led before,
Rock after rock the wheels upbore;
The careful driver slowly sped,
To many a bough we duck'd the head,
And heard the wild inviting calls
Of summer's tinkling waterfalls,
In wooded glens below; and still,
At every step the sister hill,
BLORENGE, grew greater, half unseen
At times from out our bowers of green.
That telescopic landscapes made,
From the arch'd windows of its shade;

44

For woodland tracts begirt us round;
The vale beyond was fairy ground,
That verse can never paint. Above
Gleam'd something like the mount of Jove,
(But how much let the learned say
Who take Olympus in their way)
Gleam'd the fair, sunny, cloudless peak
That simple strangers ever seek.
And are they simple? Hang the dunce
Who would not doff his cap at once
In extasy, when, bold and new,
Bursts on his sight a mountain-view.

Though vast the prospect here became,
Intensely as the love of fame
Glow'd the strong hope, that strange desire,
That deathless wish of climbing higher,
Where heather clothes his graceful sides,
Which many a scatter'd rock divides,
Bleach'd by more years than hist'ry knows,
Mov'd by no power but melting snows,
Or gushing springs, that wash away
Th' embedded earth that forms their stay.
The heart distends, the whole frame feelsr
Where, inaccessible to wheels,
The utmost storm-worn summit spreads
Its rocks grotesque, its downy beds;
Here no false feeling sense belies,
Man lifts the weary foot, and sighs;
Laughter is dumb; hilarity
Forsakes at once th' astonish'd eye;
E'en the clos'd lip, half useless grown,
Drops but a word, "Look down; look down."

GOOD Heav'ns! must scenes like these expand,
Scenes so magnificently grand,
And millions breathe, and pass away,
Unbless'd, throughout their little day,

With one short glimpse? By place confin'd,
Shall many an anxious ardent mind,
Sworn to the Muses, cow'r its pride,
Doom'd but to sing with pinions tied?

SPIRIT of BURNS! the daring child
Of glorious freedom, rough and wild,
How have I wept o'er all thy ills,
How blest thy Caledonian hills!
How almost worshipp'd in my dreams
Thy mountain haunts, — thy classic streams!
How burnt with hopeless, aimless fire,
To mark thy giant strength aspire
In patriot themes! and tun'd the while
Thy *"Bonny Doon,"* or *"Balloch Mile."*
Spirit of BURNS! accept the tear
That rapture gives thy mem'ry here
On the bleak mountain top. Here thou
Thyself had rais'd the gallant brow
Of conscious intellect, to twine
Th'imperishable verse of thine,
That charm'st the world. Or can it be,
That scenes like these were nought to thee?
That Scottish hills so far excel,
That so deep sinks the Scottish dell,
That boasted PEN-Y-VALE had been[1],
For thy loud northern lyre too mean;
[Footnote 1: The respective heights of these mountains above the
mouth of
the Gavany, was taken barometrically by General Roy.
                    Feet
The summit of the Sugar-Loaf……….1852
Of the Blorenge…………………...1720
Of the Skyrid…………………….1498]
Broad-shoulder'd BLORENGE a mere knoll,
And SKYRID, let him smile or scowl,
A dwarfish bully, vainly proud
Because he breaks the passing cloud?

If even so, thou bard of fame,
The consequences rest the same:
For, grant that to thy infant sight
Rose mountains of stupendous height;
Or grant that Cambrian minstrels taught
'Mid scenes that mock the lowland thought;
Grant that old TALLIESIN flung
His thousand raptures, as he sung
From huge PLYNLIMON'S awful brow,
Or CADER IDRIS, capt with snow;
Such Alpine scenes with them or thee
Well suited. — *These* are Alps to me.

LONG did we, noble BLORENGE, gaze
On thee, and mark the eddying haze
That strove to reach thy level crown,
From the rich stream, and smoking town;
And oft, old SKYRID, hail'd thy name,
Nor dar'd deride thy holy fame[1].
[Footnote 1: There still remains, on the summit of the Skyrid, or St.
Michael's Mount, the foundation of an ancient chapel, to which the
inhabitants formerly ascended on Michaelmas Eve, in a kind of
pilgrimage.
A prodigious cleft, or separation in the hill, tradition says, was
caused
by the earthquake at the crucifixion, it was therefore termed the
Holy
Mountain.]
Long follow'd with untiring eye
Th' illumin'd clouds, that o'er the sky
Drew their thin veil, and slowly sped,
Dipping to every mountain's head,
Dark-mingling, fading, wild, and thence,
Till admiration, in suspense,
Hung on the verge of sight. Then sprung,
By thousands known, by thousands sung,
Feelings that earth and time defy,

That cleave to immortality.

A light gray haze enclos'd us round;
Some momentary drops were found,
Borne on the breeze; soon all dispell'd;
Once more the glorious prospect swell'd
Interminably fair[1]. Again
[Footnote 1: This hill commands a view of the counties of Radnor,
Salop,
Brecknock, Glamorgan, Hereford, Worcester, Gloucester, Somerset,
and
Wilts.]
Stretch'd the BLACK MOUNTAIN'S dreary chain!
When eastward turn'd the straining eye,
Great MALVERN met the cloudless sky:
Southward arose th'embattled shores,
Where Ocean in his fury roars,
And rolls abrupt his fearful tides,
Far still from MENDIP'S fern-clad sides;
From whose vast range of mingling blue,
The weary, wand'ring sight withdrew,
O'er fair GLAMORGAN'S woods and downs,
O'er glitt'ring streams, and farms, and towns,
Back to the TABLE ROCK, that lours
O'er old CRICKHOWEL'S ruin'd towers.

Here perfect stillness reign'd. The breath
A moment hush'd, 'twas mimic death.
The ear, from all assaults releas'd,
As motion, sound, and life, had ceas'd.
The beetle rarely murmur'd by,
No sheep-dog sent his voice so high,
Save when, by chance, far down the steep,
Crept a live speck, a straggling sheep;
Yet one lone object, plainly seen,
Curv'd slowly, in a line of green,
On the brown heath: no demon fell,
No wizard foe, with magic spell,

To chain the senses, chill the heart,
No wizard guided POWEL'S cart;
He of our nectar had the care,
All our ambrosia rested there.
At leisure, but reluctant still,
We join'd him by a mountain rill;
And there, on springing turf, all seated,
Jove's guests were never half so treated;
Journies they had, and feastings many,
But never came to ABERGANY;
Lucky escape: — the wrangling crew,
Mischief to cherish, or to brew,
Was all their sport: and when, in rage,
They chose 'midst warriors to engage,
"Our chariots of fire," they cried,
And dash'd the gates of heav'n aside,
Whirl'd through the air, and foremost stood
'Midst mortal passions, mortal blood,
Celestial power with earthly mix'd;
Gods by the arrow's point transfix'd!
Beneath us frown'd no deadly war,
And POWEL'S wheels were safer far;
As on them, without flame or shield,
Or bow to twang, or lance to wield,
We left the heights of inspiration,
And relish'd a mere mortal station;
Our object, not to fire a town,
Or aid a chief, or knock him down;
But safe to sleep from war and sorrow,
And drive to BRECKNOCK on the morrow.

HEAVY and low'ring, crouds on crouds,
Drove adverse hosts of dark'ning clouds
Low o'er the vale, and far away,
Deep gloom o'erspread the rising day;
No morning beauties caught the eye,
O'er mountain top, or stream, or sky,
As round the castle's ruin'd tower,

We mus'd for many a solemn hour;
And, half-dejected, half in spleen,
Computed idly, o'er the scene,
How many murders there had dy'd
Chiefs and their minions, slaves of pride;
When perjury, in every breath,
Pluck'd the huge falchion from its sheath,
And prompted deeds of ghastly fame,
That hist'ry's self might blush to name[1].
[Footnote 1: In Jones's History of Brecknockshire, the castle of
Abergavenny is noticed as having been the scene of the most shock-
ing
enormities.]

At length, through each retreating shower,
Burst, with a renovating power,
Light, life, and gladness; instant fled
All contemplations on the dead.

Who hath not mark'd, with inward joy,
The efforts of the diving boy;
And, waiting while he disappear'd,
Exulted, trembled, hop'd, and fear'd?
Then felt his heart, 'midst cheering cries,
Bound with delight to see him rise?
Who hath not burnt with rage, to see
Falshood's vile cant, and supple knee;
Then hail'd, on some courageous brow,
The power that works her overthrow;
That, swift as lightning, seals her doom,
With, "Miscreant vanish! — truth is come?"
So PEN-Y-VALE upheav'd his brow,
And left the world of fog below;
So SKYRID, smiling, broke his way
To glories of the conqu'ring day;
With matchless grace, and giant pride.
So BLORENGE turn'd the clouds aside,
And warn'd us, not a whit too soon,

To chase the flying car of noon,
Where herds and flocks unnumber'd fed,
Where USK her wand'ring mazes led.

Here on the mind, with powerful sway,
Press'd the bright joys of yesterday;
For still, though doom'd no more t'inhale
The mountain air of PEN-Y-VALE,
His broad dark-skirting woods o'erhung
Cottage and farm, where careless sung
The labourer, where the gazing steer
Low'd to the mountains, deep and clear.

SLOW less'ning BLORENGE, left behind,
Reluctantly his claims resign'd,
And stretch'd his glowing front entire,
As forward peep'd CRICKHOWEL spire;
But no proud castle turrets gleam'd;
No warrior Earl's gay banner stream'd;
E'en of thy palace, grief to tell!
A tower without a dinner bell;
An arch where jav'lin'd centries bow'd
Low to their chief, or fed the croud,
Are all that mark where once a train
Of *barons* grac'd thy rich domain,
Illustrious PEMBROKE[1]! drain'd thy bowl,
[Footnote 1: Part of the original palace of the powerful Earls of
Pembroke
is still undemolished by time.]
And caught the nobleness of soul
The harp-inspir'd, indignant blood
That prompts to arms and hardihood.

To muse upon the days gone by,
Where desolation meets the eye,
Is double life; truth, cheaply bought,
The nurse of sense, the food of thought,

Whence judgment, ripen'd, forms, at will,
Her estimates of good or ill;
And brings contrasted scenes to view,
And weighs the *old* rogues with the *new*;
Imperious tyrants, gone to dust,
With tyrants whom the world hath curs'd
Through modern ages. By what power
Rose the strong walls of old THE TOWER?
Deep in the valley, whose clear rill
Then stole through wilds, and wanders still
Through village shades, unstain'd with gore,
Where war-steeds bathe their hoofs no more.
Empires have fallen, armies bled,
Since yon old wall, with upright head,
Met the loud tempest; who can trace
When first the rude mass, from its base,
Stoop'd in that dreadful form? E'en thou,
JANE, with the placid silver brow,
Know'st not the day, though thou hast seen
An hundred[1] springs of cheerful green,
[Footnote 1: Jane Edwards, or as she pronounced it, *Etwarts*, a tall,
bony, upright woman, leaning both hands on the head of her stick,
and in
her manners venerably impressive, was then at the age of one hun-
dred. She
was living in 1809, then one hundred and two.]
An hundred winters' snows increase
That brook, the emblem of thy peace.
Most venerable dame! and shall
The plund'rer, in his gorgeous hall,
His fame, with Moloch-frown prefer,
And scorn *thy* harmless character?
Who scarcely hear'st of his renown,
And never sack'd nor burnt a town;
But should he crave, with coward cries,
To be Jane Edwards when he dies,
Thou'lt be the conqueror, old lass,
So take thy alms, and let us pass.

FORTH from the calm sequester'd shade,
Once more approaching twilight bade;
When, as the sigh of joy arose,
And while e'en fancy sought repose,
One vast transcendent object sprung,
Arresting every eye and tongue;
Strangers, fair BRECON, wondering, scan
The peaks of thy stupendous VANN:
But how can strangers, chain'd by time,
Through floating clouds his summit climb?
Another day had almost fled;
A clear horizon, glowing red,
Its promise on all hearts impress'd,
Bright sunny hours, and Sabbath rest.

END OF THE THIRD BOOK.

BOOK IV.

CONTENTS OF BOOK IV.

The Gaer, a Roman Station.—Brunless Castle.—The Hay.—Funeral Song, "Mary's Grave."—Clifford Castle.—Return by Hereford, Malvern Hills, Cheltenham, and Gloucester, to Uley.—Conclusion.

BOOK IV.

'Tis sweet to hear the soothing chime,
And, by thanksgiving, measure time;
When hard-wrought poverty awhile
Upheaves the bending back to smile;
When servants hail, with boundless glee,
The sweets of love and liberty;
For guiltless love will ne'er disown
The cheerful Sunday's market town,
Clean, silent, when his power's confess'd,
And trade's contention lull'd to rest.

Seldom has worship cheer'd my soul
With such invincible controul!
It was a bright benignant hour,
The song of praise was full of power;
And, darting from the noon-day sky,
Amidst the tide of harmony,
O'er aisle and pillar glancing strong,
Heav'ns radiant light inspir'd the song.
The word of peace, that can disarm
Care with its own peculiar charm,
Here flow'd a double stream, to cheer
The Saxon[1] and the Mountaineer,
[Footnote 1: Divine service is performed alternately in English and
Welsh.
That they still call us Saxons, need hardly be mentioned. I observed
the
army to be equally as accommodating as the church, for the posting-
bills,
for recruits, are printed in both languages.]
Of various stock, of various name,

Now join'd in rites, and join'd in fame.

YE who religion's duty teach,
What constitutes a Sabbath breach?
Is it, when joy the bosom fills,
To wander o'er the breezy hills?
Is it, to trace around your home
The footsteps of imperial Rome?
Then guilty, guilty let us plead,
Who, on the cheerful rested steed,
In thought absorb'd, explor'd, with care,
The wild lanes round the silent GAER[1],
[Footnote 1: A road must have led from Abergavenny, through the Vale of
the Usk, north-west to the "Gaer," situated two miles north-west of
Brecon, on a gentle eminence, at the conflux of the rivers Esker and
Usk.
Mr. Wyndham traced parts of walls, which he describes as exactly
resembling those at Caerleon; and Mr. Lemon found several bricks,
bearing
the inscription of LEG. II. AVG. — *Coxe.*
In addition to the above, it may be acceptable to state, that Mr.
Price, a
very intelligent farmer on the spot, has in his possession several of
the
above kind of bricks, bearing the same inscription, done, evidently,
by
stamping the clay, while moist, with an instrument. These have
been turned
up by the plough, together with several small Roman lamps.]
Where conqu'ring eagles took their stand;
Where heathen altars stain'd the land;
Where soldiers of AUGUSTUS pin'd,
Perhaps, for pleasures left behind,
And measur'd, from this lone abode,
The new-form'd, stoney, forest road,
Back to CAERLEON'S southern train,
Their barks, their home, beyond the main;

Still by the VANN reminded strong
Of Alpine scenes, and mountain song,
The olive groves, and cloudless sky,
And golden vales of Italy.

[Illustration: VAN MOUNTAIN, near BRECKNOCK from the PRIORY WOODS.]

With us 'twas peace, we met no foes;
With us far diff'rent feelings rose.
Still onward inclination bade;
The wilds of MONA'S Druid shade,
SNOWDON'S sublime and stormy brow,
His land of Britons stretch'd below,
And PENMAN MAWR'S huge crags, that greet
The thund'ring ocean at his feet,
Were all before us. Hard it prov'd,
To quit a land so dearly lov'd;
Forego each bold terrific boast
Of northern Cambria's giant coast.
Friends of the harp and song, forgive
The deep regret that, whilst I live,
Shall dwell upon my heart and tongue;
Go, joys untasted, themes unsung,
Another scene, another land,
Hence shall the homeward verse demand.
Yet fancy wove her flow'ry chain,
Till "farewell BRECON" left a pain;
A pain that travellers may endure,
Change is their food, and change their cure.
Yet, oh, how dream-like, far away,
To recollect so bright a day!
Dream-like those scenes the townsmen love,
Their tumbling USK, their PRIORY GROVE,
View'd while the moon cheer'd, calmly bright,
The freshness of a summer's night.

HIGH o'er the town, in morning smiles,
The blue VANN heav'd his deep defiles;
And rang'd, like champions for the fight,
Basking in sun-beams on our right,
Rose the BLACK MOUNTAINS, that surround
That far-fam'd spot of holy ground,
LLANTHONY, dear to monkish tale,
And still the pride of EWAIS VALE.
No road-side cottage smoke was seen,
Or rarely, on the village green
No youths appear'd, in spring-tide dress,
In ardent play, or idleness.
Brown way'd the harvest, dale and slope
Exulting bore a nation's hope;
Sheaves rose as far as sight could range,
And every mile was but a change
Of peasants lab'ring, lab'ring still,
And climbing many a distant hill.
Some talk'd, perhaps, of spring's bright hour,
And how they pil'd, in BRUNLESS TOWER [1],
[Footnote 1: The only remaining tower of Brunless Castle now makes an
excellent hay-loft; and almost every building on the spot is com-
posed of
fragments.]
The full-dried hay. Perhaps they told
Tradition's tales, and taught how old
The ruin'd castle! False or true,
They guess it, just as others do.

Lone tower! though suffer'd yet to stand,
Dilapidation's wasting hand
Shall tear thy pond'rous walls, to guard
The slumb'ring steed, or fence the yard;
Or wheels shall grind thy pride away
Along the turnpike road to HAY,
Where fierce GLENDOW'R'S rude mountaineers
Left war's attendants, blood and tears,

And spread their terrors many a mile,
And shouted round the flaming pile.
May heav'n preserve our native land
From blind ambition's murdering hand;
From all the wrongs that can provoke
A people's wrath, and urge the stroke
That shakes the proudest throne! Guard, heav'n.
The sacred birth-right thou hast given;
Bid justice curb, with strong controul,
The desp'rate passions of the soul.

Here ivy'd fragments, lowering, throw
Broad shadows on the poor below,
Who, while they rest, and when they die,
Sleep on the rock-built shores of WYE.

To tread o'er nameless mounds of earth,
To muse upon departed worth,
To credit still the poor distress'd,
For feelings never half express'd,
Their hopes, their faith, their tender love,
Faith that sustain'd, and hope that strove,
Is sacred joy; to heave a sigh,
A debt to poor mortality.
Funereal rites are clos'd; 'tis done;
Ceas'd is the bell; the priest is gone;
What then if bust or stone denies
To catch the pensive loit'rer's eyes,
What course can poverty pursue?
What can the *poor* pretend to do?
O boast not, quarries, of your store;
Boast not, O man, of wealth or lore,
The flowers of nature here shall thrive,
Affection keep those flowers alive;
And they shall strike the melting heart,
Beyond the utmost power of art;
Planted on graves[1], their stems entwine,
And every blossom is a line

[Footnote 1: To the custom of scattering flowers over the graves of
departed friends, David ap Gwillym beautifully alludes in one of
his odes.
"O whilst thy season of flowers, and thy tender sprays thick of
leaves
remain, I will pluck the roses from the brakes, the flowerets of the
meads, and gems of the wood; the vivid trefoil, beauties of the
ground,
and the gaily-smiling bloom of the verdant herbs, to be offered to
the
memory of a chief of fairest fame. Humbly will I lay them on the
grave of
Iver."
On a grave in the church-yard at Hay, or the Hay, as it is commonly
spoken, flowers had evidently been *planted*, but only one solitary
sprig
of sweet-briar had taken root.]
Indelibly impress'd, that tends,
In more than language comprehends,
To teach us, in our solemn hours,
That we ourselves are dying flowers.

What if a father buried here
His earthly hope, his friend most dear,
His only child? Shall his dim eye,
At poverty's command, be dry?
No, he shall muse, and think, and pray,
And weep his tedious hours away;
Or weave the song of woe to tell,
How dear that child he lov'd so well.

MARY'S GRAVE.

No child have I left, I must wander alone,
  No light-hearted Mary to sing as I go,
Nor loiter to gather bright flowers newly blown,

She delighted, sweet maid, in these emblems of woe.

Then the stream glided by her, or playfully boil'd
  O'er its rock-bed unceasing, and still it goes free;
But her infant life was arrested, unsoil'd
  As the dew-drop when shook by the wing of the bee.

Sweet flowers were her treasures, and flowers shall be mine;
  I bring them from Radnor's green hills to her grave;
Thus planted in anguish, oh let them entwine
  O'er a heart once as gentle as heav'n e'er gave.
Oh, the glance of her eye, when at mansions of wealth
  I pointed, suspicious, and warn'd her of harm;
She smil'd in content, 'midst the bloom of her health,
  And closer and closer still hung on my arm.

What boots it to tell of the sense she possess'd,
  The fair buds of promise that mem'ry endears?
The mild dove, affection, was queen of her breast,
  And I had her love, and her truth, and her tears;
She was mine. But she goes to the land of the good,
  A change which I must, and yet dare not deplore;
I'll bear the rude shock like the oak of the wood,
  But the green hills of Radnor will charm me no more.

RUINS of greatness, all farewell;
No Chepstows here, no Raglands tell,
By mound, or foss, or mighty tower,
Achievements high in hall or bower;
Or give to fancy's vivid eye,
The helms and plumes of chivalry.
CLIFFORD has fall'n, howe'er sublime,
Mere fragments wrestle still with time;
Yet as they perish, sure and slow,
And rolling dash the stream below,
They raise tradition's glowing scene,
The clue of silk, the wrathful queen,

And link, in mem'ry's firmest bond,
The love-lorn tale of Rosamond[1].
[Footnote 1: Clifford Castle is supposed to have been the birth place of
Fair Rosamond.]

How placid, how divinely sweet,
The flow'r-grown brook that, by our feet,
Winds on a summer's day; e'en where
Its name no classic honours share,
Its springs untrac'd, its course unknown,
Seaward for ever rambling down!
Here, then, how sweet, pelucid, chaste;
'Twas this bright current bade us taste
The fulness of its joy. Glide still,
Enchantress of PLYNLIMON HILL,
Meandering WYE! Still let me dream,
In raptures, o'er thy infant stream;
For could th' immortal soul forego
Its cumbrous load of earthly woe,
And clothe itself in fairy guise,
Too small, too pure, for human eyes,
Blithe would we seek thy utmost spring,
Where mountain-larks first try the wing;
There, at the crimson dawn of day,
Launch a scoop'd leaf, and sail away,
Stretch'd at our ease, or crouch below,
Or climb the green transparent prow,
Stooping where oft the blue bell sips
The passing stream, and shakes and dips;
And when the heifer came to drink,
Quick from the gale our bark would shrink,
And huddle down amidst the brawl
Of many a five-inch waterfall,
Till the expanse should fairly give
The bow'ring hazel room to live;
And as each swelling junction came,
To form a riv'let worth a name,

We'd dart beneath, or brush away
Long-beaded webs, that else might stay
Our silent course; in haste retreat,
Where whirlpools near the bull-rush meet;
Wheel round the ox of monstrous size;
And count below his shadowy flies;
And sport amidst the throng; and when
We met the barks of giant men,
Avoid their oars, still undescried,
And mock their overbearing pride;
Then vanish by some magic spell,
And shout, "Delicious WYE, farewell!"

'Twas noon, when o'er thy mountain stream,
The carriage roll'd, each pow'rful gleam
Struck on thy surface, where, below,
Spread the deep heaven's azure glow;
And water-flowers, a mingling croud,
Wav'd in the dazzling silver cloud.
Again farewell! The treat is o'er;
For me shall Cambria smile no more;
Yet truth shall still the song sustain,
And touch the springs of joy again.

Hail! land of cyder, vales of health!
Redundant fruitage, rural wealth;
Here, did *Pomona* still retain,
Her influence o'er a British plain,
Might temples rise, spring blossoms fly,
Round the capricious deity;
Or autumn sacrifices bound,
By myriads, o'er the hallow'd ground,
And deep libations still renew
The fervours of her dancing crew.
Land of delight! let mem'ry strive
To keep thy flying scenes alive;
Thy grey-limb'd orchards, scattering wide
Their treasures by the highway side;

Thy half-hid cottages, that show
The dark green moss, the resting bough,
At broken panes, that taps and flies,
Illumes and shades the maiden's eyes
At day-break, and, with whisper'd joy,
Wakes the light-hearted shepherd boy:
These, with thy noble woods and dells,
The hazel copse, the village bells,
Charm'd more the passing sultry hours
Than HEREFORD, with all her towers.

Sweet was the rest, with welcome cheer,
But a far nobler scene was near;
And when the morrow's noon had spread,
O'er orchard stores, the deep'ning red,
Behind us rose the billowy cloud,
That dims the air to city croud.

And deem not that, where cyder reigns
The beverage of a thousand plains,
Malt, and the liberal harvest horn,
Are all unknown, or laugh'd to scorn;
A spot that all delights might bring,
A palace for an eastern king,
CANFROME[A], shall from her vaults display
John Barleycorn's resistless sway.
[Footnote A: The noble seat of—Hopton, Esq. which exhibits, in a striking
manner, the real old English magnificence and hospitality of the last
age.]
To make the odds of fortune even,
Up bounc'd the cork of *seventy-seven,*"
And sent me back to school; for then,
Ere yet I learn'd to wield the pen;
The pen that should all crimes assail,
The pen that leads to fame—or jail;
Then steem'd the malt, whose spirit bears

The frosts and suns of thirty years!

Through LEDBURY, at decline of day,
The wheels that bore us, roll'd away,
To cross the MALVERN HILLS. 'Twas night;
Alternate met the weary sight
Each steep, dark, undulating brow,
And WORC'STER'S gloomy vale below:
Gloomy no more, when eastward sprung
The light that gladdens heart and tongue;
When morn glanc'd o'er the shepherd's bed,
And cast her tints of lovely red
Wide o'er the vast expanding scene,
And mix'd her hues with mountain green;
Then, gazing from a height so fair,
Through miles of unpolluted air,
Where cultivation triumphs wide,
O'er boundless views on every side,
Thick planted towns, where toils ne'er cease,
And far-spread silent village peace,
As each succeeding pleasure came,
The heart acknowledg'd MALVERN'S fame.

Oft glancing thence to Cambria still,
Thou yet wert seen, my fav'rite hill,
Delightful PEN-Y-VALE! Nor shall
Great MALVERN'S high imperious call
Wean me from thee, or turn aside
My earliest charm, my heart's strong pride.

Boast MALVERN, that thy springs revive
The drooping patient, scarce alive;
Where, as he gathers strength to toil,
Not e'en thy heights his spirit foil,
But nerve him on to bless, t'inhale,
And triumph in the morning gale;
Or noon's transcendent glories give

The vigorous touch that bids him live.
Perhaps e'en now he stops to breathe,
Surveying the expanse beneath?
Now climbs again, where keen winds blow.
And holds his beaver to his brow;
Waves to the *Wrecken* his white hand,
And, borrowing Fancy's magic wand,
Skims over WORC'STER'S spires away,
Where sprung the blush of rising day;
And eyes, with joy, sweet *Hagley Groves*,
That taste reveres and virtue loves;
And stretch'd upon thy utmost ridge,
Marks Severn's course, and UPTON-bridge,
That leads to home, to friends, or wife,
And all thy sweets, domestic life;
He drops the tear, his bosom glows,
That consecrated *Avon* flows
Down the blue distant vale, to yield
Its stores by TEWKESBURY'S deadly field,
And feels whatever can inspire,
From history's page or poet's fire.

Bright vale of Severn! shall the song
That wildly devious roves along,
The charms of nature to explore,
On history rest, or themes of yore?
More joy the thoughts of home supply,
Short be the glance at days gone by,
Though gallant TEWKESBURY, clean and gay,
Hath much to tempt the traveller's stay,
Her noble abbey, with its dead,
A powerful claim; a silent dread,
Sacred as holy virtue springs
Where rests the dust of chiefs and kings;
With his who by foul murder died,
The fierce Lancastrian's hope and pride,
When brothers brothers could destroy
Heroic Margaret's *red-rose* boy.[A]

[Footnote A: Prince Edward, son of Henry the Sixth, taken prisoner
with
his mother, Margaret of Anjou, at the battle of Tewkesbury, and
murdered
by the Duke of Gloucester, afterwards Richard the Third.]
Muse, turn thee from the field of blood,
Rest to the brave, peace to the good;
Avon, with all thy charms, adieu!
For CHELTENHAM mocks thy pilgrim crew;
And like a girl in beauty's power,
Flirts in the fairings of an hour.

Queen of the valley! soon behind
Gleam'd thy bright fanes, in sun and wind,
Fair Glo'ster. Though thy fabric stands,
The boast of Severn's winding sands
If grandeur, beauty, grace, can stay
The traveller on his homeward way.
There rests the Norman prince who rose
In zeal against the Christian's foes,
Yet doom'd at home to pine and die,
Of birthright rob'd, and liberty;
Foil'd was the lance he well could fling,
Robert[A], who should have been a king;
[Footnote A: The eldest son of William the Conqueror was impris-
oned
eight-and-twenty years by his own brother!]
His tide of wrongs he could not stem,
His brothers filch'd his diadem.
There sleeps the king who aim'd to spurn
The daring Scots, at Bannockburn,
But turn'd him back, with humbled fame,
And *Berkley's "shrieks"*[B] declare his name.
[Footnote B: "Shrieks of an agonizing king."]

Cease, cease the lay, the goal is won,
But silent memory revels on;
Fast clos'd the day, the last bright hour,

The setting sun, on DURSLEY tower,
Welcom'd us home, and forward bade,
To ULEY valley's peaceful shade.

Who so unfeeling, who so bold,
To judge that fictions, idly told,
Deform the verse that only tries
To consecrate realities?
If e'er th' unworthy thought should come,
Let strong conviction strike them dumb.
Go to the proof; your steed prepare,
Drink nature's cup, the rapture share;
If dull you find your devious course,
Your tour is useless — sell your horse.

Ye who, ingulph'd in trade, endure
What gold alone can never cure;
The constant sigh for scenes of peace,
From the world's trammels free release,
Wait not, for reason's sake attend,
Wait not in chains till times shall mend;
Till the clear voice, grown hoarse and gruff,
Cries, "Now I'll go, I'm rich enough;"
Youth, and the prime of manhood, seize,
Steal ten days absence, ten days ease;
Bid ledgers from your minds depart;
Let mem'ry's treasures cheer the heart;
And when your children round you grow,
With opening charms and manly brow,
Talk of the WYE as some old dream,
Call it the wild, the wizard stream;
Sink in your broad arm-chair to rest,
And youth shall smile to see you bless'd.

Artists, betimes your powers employ,
And take the pilgrimage of joy;
The eye of genius may behold

A thousand beauties here untold;
Rock, that defies the winter's storm;
Wood, in its most imposing form,
That climbs the mountain, bows below,
Where deep th' unsullied waters flow.
Here *Gilpin's* eye transported scan'd
Views by no tricks of fancy plan'd;
Gray here, upon the stream reclin'd,
Stor'd with delight his ardent mind.
But let the vacant trifler stray
From thy enchantments far away;
For should, from fashion's rainbow train,
The idle and the vicious vain,
In sacrilege presume to move
Through these dear scenes of peace and love,
The *spirit of the stream* would rise
In wrathful mood, and tenfold size,
And nobly guard his COLDWELL SPRING,
And bid his inmost caverns ring;
Loud thund'ring on the giddy crew,
"My stream was never meant for you."
But ye, to nobler feelings born,
Who sense and nature dare not scorn.,
Glide gaily on, and ye shall find
The blest serenity of mind
That springs from silence; or shall raise
The hand, the eye, the voice of praise.
Live then, sweet stream! and henceforth be
The darling of posterity;
Lov'd for thyself, for ever dear,
Like beauty's smile and virtue's tear,
Till time his striding race give o'er,
And verse itself shall charm no more.

THE END.